THE WEDDING

The Wedding

Story Wendy Orr
Art Ruth Ohi

Annick Press

Annick Press Ltd.

Annick Press gratefully acknowledges the support of the Canada
Council and the Ontario Arts Council.

Canadian Cataloguing in Publication Data

Orr, Wendy
    The wedding

(Micki and Daniel ; 2)
ISBN 1-55037-280-7 (bound) ISBN 1-55037-281-5 (pbk.)

I. Ohi, Ruth.   II. Title.   III. Series: Orr, Wendy.
Micki and Daniel ; 2.

PS8579.R7W44 1993   jC813'.54   C92-095196-1
PZ7.077We 1993

The art in this book was rendered in watercolour. The text has been
set in Bookman Light by Attic Typesetting.

Distributed in Canada and the USA by:
Firefly Books Ltd.
250 Sparks Avenue
Willowdale, Ontario   M2H 2S4

 Printed on acid-free paper.

Printed and bound in Canada by
D.W. Friesen and Sons, Altona, Manitoba

*To who else
but Tom*

Micki
Moon
was
skinny
with
straight
dark
hair.

Daniel Day
was short and
round with curly
blond hair.

Micki's real name was Michelle, but she liked Micki better.

Daniel's real name was Daniel, and that was that.

Micki Moon liked: running, jumping, shouting, singing, dancing, windy days, big waves, tall trees, horses, jumping off haystacks, climbing high rocks, being with Daniel, and fried egg and sardine sandwiches.

Daniel Day liked: playing his violin, daydreaming, playing chess, puzzles and math, calm days, floating in warm water, watching birds, lying in long grass, sleeping in haystacks, being with Micki, and fried egg and sardine sandwiches.

Micki and Daniel had been friends for as long as they could remember. When they were babies their mothers had given them pink and blue rattles and put them on a rug to play. Later they gave Micki dolls and Daniel trucks, and Micki and Daniel put the dolls in the trucks and went off and did what they liked.

Somehow, something always seemed to happen when Micki and Daniel were together . . .

Micki and Daniel had been invited to a wedding. Micki was a flower girl and Daniel had to play his violin.

"And you cannot take Pegasus," said Micki's mother. "Ponies don't belong in weddings."

"And you cannot take Ooloo Mooloo," said Daniel's mother. Ooloo Mooloo was a parrot with a bad habit of saying the wrong thing.

"But I think we could take them," Micki said to Daniel. "They can just stay outside the church and watch."

Micki had a long pink dress with lots of lace. It was the kind of dress that she would have rather made into another nosebag for Pegasus.

She didn't mind the flowers, though: "Roses are Pegasus' favourite," she said. "After oats."

Daniel's mother wouldn't let Ooloo Mooloo ride on Daniel's shoulder to the church, so he left the window open and Ooloo Mooloo flew into the car just as they drove off.

It was hot and beautiful the day of the wedding. Micki's mother would not let her ride Pegasus to the church, so Micki gave her her nosebag and opened the gate, and she followed the car.

When they got to the church Micki put Pegasus at a little side door so she could watch, and Daniel put Ooloo Mooloo on Pegasus' back so he could listen. Then they went inside.

The wedding started. The bride looked beautiful and the groom looked handsome; the fathers looked proud and the mothers looked like they were crying. Everyone whispered that it was a perfect wedding.

Daniel started to play.

Micki watched Pegasus eating her nosebag and tried not to dance.

Ooloo Mooloo rocked on Pegasus' back—but it was no good. He flew to Pegasus' head—but it was no good.

There was only one place Ooloo Mooloo could listen to music.

The door was open just a crack. Ooloo Mooloo nudged it and pushed it and squeezed through—and flew to Daniel's shoulder.

The groom gave a gasp
and the bride turned
pink. "They must have
been getting bored," said
Micki. "They'll be glad to
have a parrot to look at."

Daniel went on playing.
Ooloo Mooloo rocked and
Micki danced a wedding
dance, and at the end of
the song Ooloo Mooloo
shouted, "Encore!
Encore!"

"Quiet, Ooloo Mooloo," Daniel whispered.

"If you keep on playing," Micki said, "he won't say anything worse."

"Encore! Encore!" shouted Ooloo Mooloo.

The people started to laugh and the bride turned pinker.

"Be quiet or I'll take you back to Pegasus," whispered Daniel, and Ooloo Mooloo was quiet.

The minister started to talk. A baby started to cry.
The minister said kindly, "Don't mind the baby—"
but as soon as he said 'baby', Ooloo Mooloo started to
wail and scream and screech and make disgusting
noises like about one hundred angry babies.

"NO, Ooloo Mooloo, no!" shouted Daniel, and Ooloo
Mooloo stopped.

The baby in the church did not stop. It was so angry at so many other babies screaming louder than it that it wailed and screamed and screeched and made even more disgusting noises than Ooloo Mooloo, and its mother had to take it outside.

The minister started again.

"Do you, Simon," he began —

"No, Ooloo Mooloo!" said Daniel. "He said 'Simon'—not—"

But Ooloo Mooloo began to wail like a fire truck siren, then an ambulance siren, and finally like a police siren, until all the people were turning around and staring and shouting and running outside in case the building was burning down.

"Ooloo Mooloo," said Daniel. "One more sound and I won't play my violin for a week!"

Ooloo Mooloo was quiet. After a while the people were quiet too. The minister started again.

Pegasus finished her nosebag. She rubbed her head on the door till the nosebag slipped off. But now the door was open a little more so she put her head in to see a little better—and her neck—and her shoulders—and somehow her tail just seemed to follow—and all of Pegasus was in the church. She could see Micki.

She thought she would go closer just to make sure.

It *was* Micki. And she was carrying—roses!

Pegasus went a little closer.

"I now pronounce you husband and wife," said the minister, and the groom kissed the bride and the bride kissed the groom. Then the bride and groom, and Daniel and his violin and Ooloo Mooloo, and Micki and the roses started down the aisle.

Pegasus followed. She knew those roses were for her, but she didn't want Micki to forget.

The bride and groom stood on the church steps so all the people could shake their hands and say how lucky they were and what a beautiful wedding it had been.

The people did not seem to think Pegasus should be on the church steps with the bride and groom. "Shoo!" they said. "Shoo! Get out!"

Pegasus went down the steps slowly. She did not like people saying 'Shoo! Get out!' She stopped at the bottom of the steps and would not go any farther.

It was hard to push Pegasus when she did not want to move, and the people soon decided she had gone far enough.

"Poor Pegasus!" said Micki, and fed her the roses from her bouquet one by one. Pegasus ate them and looked as happy as a round shaggy pony can look.

Ooloo Mooloo sat on Daniel's shoulder and pecked at his ear and said "More, more!" until Daniel had fed him all the fried egg and sardine sandwiches in his pocket.

The people went on telling the bride how beautiful she was and the groom how handsome he was—though they didn't sound very sure any more about the perfect wedding.

"Throw your bouquet!" the people called to the bride. "Throw it to me! Throw it to me!" And all the girls and women who wanted good luck or good husbands crowded forward to catch the bouquet.

The bride lifted her bouquet.

"ROSES!" thought Pegasus, and all the girls who wanted good luck or good husbands were knocked flying and—

CHOMP!

And when the bride stopped crying and the groom stopped shouting, the people told them again how lucky they were, and how beautiful they were, and what a very special wedding it had been.

"It wasn't that special," Micki said. "Nothing much happened. I'm never having a wedding."

"I might," said Daniel. "If I could play the music and have Ooloo Mooloo. I might have lots."

"Maybe just one," said Micki. "As long as I could dance and there were lots of roses for Pegasus."